I0771602

The Scriptures of Mary Magdalene

by

Mary-Eisa

This heartwarming novel explores the captivating journey of Seraphina, a renowned historical researcher who profoundly desires to understand Mary Magdalene's heart. Through actual research, what could she uncover about the woman with unwavering faith who was guided fearlessly to dedicate her life to spreading the message of Jesus and creating the inception of Christianity?

Seraphina's journey takes an exciting and mystical turn when a mysterious woman emerges from the depths of papyrus pages and ancient books, leaving her breathless. As the narrative unfolds, Seraphina embarks on an extraordinary quest, from exploring the recently excavated town of Magdala to visiting the ancient site of Sainte-Baume.

Seraphina's adventure is nothing short of breathtaking. Enhanced by the complete Gospel of Mary and the Manichaean Psalms of Heracleids, the story deepens as Seraphina reaches out to connect with the timeless spirit she has yearned to comprehend more fully. With its vibrant storytelling and thorough research, *The Scriptures of Mary Magdalene* invites readers to reevaluate the historical and spiritual significance of a woman whose influence continues to resonate through the ages.

This exciting fictional novel, based on historical records and scrolls, is a literary journey filled with breathtaking moments, like a sweeping vista of a distant land, profound insights, and a whisper from Mary Magdalene's long-lost soul.

Books by this same author

Finding God's Goodness

Love Puts Things Right

The Scriptures of Mary Magdalene

The Scriptures of Mary Magdalene

Copyright © 2025 by Mary-Eisa Yee. All rights reserved, printed in the United States of America. No part of this book may be used or reproduced in any manner whatsoever without written permission except for brief quotations embedded in critical articles and reviews.

Mary-Eisa website: http//:www.mary-eisa.com

ISBN: paperback: 979-8-9896958-1-2

ISBN: ebook: 979-8-9896958-2-9

Cover by: Mary -Eisa

As you delve into these pages, I sincerely hope they serve as a testament to the enduring faith and deep affection held for Mary Magdalene.

Contents

The Scriptures of Mary Magdalene.

To begin—

Our story unfolds in a New England village, a place of such enchanting beauty that it seems to have been plucked from a fairytale. Here, a beautifully preserved Federal-style residence stands as a hidden gem. The home is nestled within a dense pine forest, surrounded by the refreshing scent of pine and the invigorating aroma of evergreens. The front entrance boasts majestic columns and a fanlight entryway, welcoming guests with a touch of grandeur. Sunlight streams through the generous windows, enveloping every room in a soothing, ethereal glow as delicate lace curtains cast enchanting shadows on the walls.

In the grand confines of this stately home resides a woman named Seraphina. Despite Seraphina's father being absent, he left behind a meaningful legacy in the form of his life's work for his cherished wife and daughter and her beautiful name. Overwhelmed with happiness when he first cradled her in his arms, a beaming smile illuminated his face as he joyfully declared, "Her name is Seraphina." In complete agreement, Seraphina's mother lovingly gazed at their newborn daughter, feeling that "Seraphina" would perfectly capture their little girl's spirit—a name that resonated with grace, purity, and an undeniable light that shone within this tiny bundle of joy.

And so our story begins with Seraphina, a woman of petite stature but immense and perspicuous intellect, who now shares this home with her beloved best friend and mother, Annah. Together, their presence fills the house with a harmonious blend of care and a relentless thirst for knowledge, a bond that warms the very walls of their home.

Seraphina has established herself as a distinguished, well-degreed historical researcher, a Historian known for unearthing the most obscure fragments of information from the depths of time. Her days are a testament to her unwavering passion, filled with a relentless pursuit of projects for prestigious global enterprises and universities around the world. In her workspace, meticulously crafted notes and reports cover every available surface, a testament to her dedication and love for her craft.

Her workspace, affectionately known as the Long Room, is a long, narrow space that spans the entire length of the dwelling. The room is steeped in the scent of aged walnut, mingling with the faint aroma of old pages and leather bindings. The site is a marvel, with floor-to-ceiling bookshelves crafted from intricately carved rich wood. These shelves house a treasure trove of priceless historical books, their worn spines and yellowed pages whispering of the long-ago stories they hold. The room, a legacy from Seraphina's father, an eminent historian, instantly captivates you, leaving a yearning to delve into the tales contained within those aged volumes. At the heart of the Long Room, a cozy sitting area beckons, complete with a step-chair for reaching the higher shelves and a soft leather chair where Seraphina spends hours reading. The room's centerpiece is a set of elaborate 17th-century Italian hand-carved walnut tables, each stacked with a treasure trove of rare manuscripts, papyrus-bound codexes, and scrolls, a testament to its rich history and knowledge.

The Long Room is a precious, rare, and cherished library with a special place in Seraphina's heart. Her father, an ardent collector of antique books, painstakingly curated this now-valuable collection of ancient texts. As a young girl, she joined her father on many of his expeditions to remote and exotic locations. These travels began her deep appreciation for ancient books, sparking a lifelong passion for research and discovery. The lure of ancient texts and hidden secrets would continue to take her on long journeys worldwide and back again. As she enters the Long Room, a rush of memories engulfs her, her father's presence almost tangible. The room is brimming with his love for knowledge and hidden histories. The air carries the faint scent of aged books while the soft sound of turning pages whispers in her ears. As memories of her father's love flood her mind, Seraphina feels a surge of emotions, as if he were still beside her.

She loves sitting at her father's old desk, the one he spent countless hours at, lost in his thoughts and ideas. The desk was a testament to his curiosity and creativity, cluttered with papers, notebooks, and a vintage typewriter that still works perfectly. She feels it is magical, connecting her to her father when she types out her thoughts and research notes on the same keys he once touched. In this room, filled with her father's books and notes, Seraphina feels an overwhelming sense of connection to a higher purpose, carrying on her father's intellectual legacy and embracing the profound joy of being a part of something she feels is genuinely extraordinary.

An indescribable warmth from her loving mother, Annah, creates an irreplaceable essence in every corner of their home. Her nurturing spirit is the cornerstone of their household, filling it with peace and serenity. Annah is also a passionate book lover who is retired from teaching but continues to contribute her time by assisting at the nearby university library. Seraphina's mother, a native of the beautiful New England coast, has a voice reflecting the distinctive long "R" accent of her Boston upbringing. This warm and familiar accent reminds Seraphina of cozy family gatherings and the region's vibrant culture. Meanwhile, her father, born in the historic city of

Newcastle in the United Kingdom, spoke with a deep and rich Geordie accent. His speech was marked by a musical lilt and a hearty cadence that painted vivid images of the rugged northern landscapes he had known. Seraphina adored the moments when her parents engaged in conversation. Their contrasting accents intertwined beautifully, creating a unique harmony echoing their diverse backgrounds brought to the family. The blend of her mother's New England charm and her father's Geordie warmth sparked every conversation with a delightful worldly flair, connecting her to their rich tapestry of shared experiences and traditions.

Annah finds immense joy in the farmhouse-style kitchen, awash in her favorite calming hues of soft blues, delicately complemented by accents of white and soft beige tones. It is a sanctuary where she can lose herself for hours, skillfully preparing mouthwatering vegetarian dishes for her and her daughter to enjoy.

Joseph, a highly skilled gardener, and beloved family friend, is a cherished part of their family. He maintains their garden, creating all the needed vegetables, lettuce, and aromatic herbs for Annah's luscious dishes. His craft and tender care are evident in the impressive yearly produce generously shared throughout the neighboring community.

While their beautiful home is full of joy and inspiration, Seraphina has hidden an unfulfilled longing and passion. While she takes great satisfaction in her daily work and finds joy in her routine, this hidden longing lingers beneath the surface, coloring her thoughts and shaping her dreams. It is this hidden passion that lies at the heart of our story.

After what felt like an eternity of academic responsibilities, Seraphina has finally found the chance to embark on a passionate quest. She is eager to explore her secret passion: delving into the history and essence of a woman she has long admired—the mysterious and legendary Mary Magdalene.

Her fascination with Mary Magdalene blossomed during her childhood Bible study classes. It reached its pinnacle when she delved into the passage where Mary, with a desperate plea, found the tomb empty and asked for the body of her beloved Lord: "If you have taken him away, tell me where you have put him, and I will go and get him." (John 20:13-16) As Seraphina immersed herself in those words, she fell back in time, surrounded by the scene's sights, sounds, and emotions. She imagined the heavy weight of despair that must have filled the air. Having personally experienced the anguish of losing a loved one when her father passed away unexpectedly, she truly understood Mary's sorrow. She pictured Mary standing there, her trembling hands clutching the folds of her dress, completely overwhelmed by grief. Seraphina could almost feel the quiver in Mary's voice reverberating through her body. Mary's unwavering courage and determination shone through even in the face of fear that caused the men to scatter in all directions. Yet, her voice cut through any fear, commanding attention and respect. Mary's enigmatic persona and eyes filled with sorrow and fierce determination reminded Seraphina that it would not be just anyone who could ask where her beloved was and possess the authority to retrieve him. This plea, recorded in the Bible, was a remarkable validation of Mary's status and proof of her relationship with Jesus. Then, through the blur of tears, Seraphina could easily understand Mary's struggle to recognize Jesus, mistaking him for a gardener. But as soon as she heard his gentle, rich voice utter, "Woman, why are you crying?" a wave of familiarity washed over her. At that instant, a profound sense of relief enveloped her as she called out, "Rabbouni,"

Over the years, Seraphina became even more determined to discover the genuine essence and belief in Jesus that this extraordinary woman, the Magdala—Mary Magdalene—or, in French, Marie Madeleine, possessed.

Now that the opportunity had arrived, she was anxious to delve deeper into what historical information she could find to understand Mary Magdalene's heart and devotion to Jesus. She hoped to unravel the intricate threads that shaped her into a woman with such deep understanding and unwavering faith, and her knowledge shrouded in darkness for centuries.

Throughout her travels and studies, she gathered as much information as possible through books, notes, copies of scrolls, codexes, and various papers and travels. She took great care to catalog and organize everything she could find systematically, placing them all in a large box where one day she would begin her mission to put everything gathered together to uncover as much of the truth as she could about the story of the woman who is said in the Gnostic Gospel "Dialogue of the Savior," as the woman who understood and knew it all — Mary Magdalene.

On this evening, she couldn't help but feel excitement and anticipation as she gazed down at the large box before her. Tomorrow, she would start. With a contented smile playing on her lips, she made a silent vow to greet the early morning hours. But now, as the sun dipped below the horizon, casting a warm glow across the sky, she relished the tranquil ambiance of the evening twilight. Savoring the last sip of her fragrant tea and exchanging a heartfelt goodnight with her mother, she dreamily retired to her bedroom. The softness of her favorite blanket enveloped her, wrapping her in comfort as she settled into a peaceful slumber, eagerly awaiting the promise the new day held for her.

Chapter One

In Her Voice—Mary Magdalene

Annah's cheerful voice echoed through the house as she called to Seraphina from downstairs. "Good morning, Darling! Are you working today?" she asks, her tone full of curiosity.

Seraphina's eyes reluctantly tore away from the pages of her book as her attention was drawn to her mother's voice, which echoed through the house. "No, Mum. I have the day to myself, and I will enjoy reading."

"All right then," Annah says affectionately, "I will leave you with your reading and see you later for supper. Bye, dear." As she heard the downstairs door softly close, she couldn't help but feel a sense of peace wash over her.

Earlier, while her mother was still peacefully slumbering, Seraphina had tiptoed away to her cherished sanctuary upstairs, a haven that had brought her immense joy during her younger years. The room exuded a sense of tranquility, with its pale lavender walls adorned with delicate paintings and shelves filled with cherished mementos. As she settled into the cozy armchair, she relished the familiar creak of the floorboards beneath her feet, transporting her back to her childhood days. The room was situated on the highest floor of the home, affording a spectacular view of the lush gardens below and a small lake that seemed to merge seamlessly into the horizon. Whenever she craved solitude, she would retreat to this refuge, where she would be surrounded by the books she loved and the familiar embrace of a favorite old chair that had once belonged to her grandmother. The room was a veritable time capsule, with a worn record player that could still whisper songs transporting her back to childhood days.

Outside, the rain cascaded down in a gentle, rhythmic pattern, creating a blissful, comforting melody as she sank into the warm embrace of her grandmother's beloved chair. Its tattered fabric was a testament to the countless hours lost in its comfort, allowing a wave of continued nostalgia to wash over her. As she settled down to read the contents of her box, Seraphina carefully placed an antique writing and reading board over the broad arms of the chair. The board, made of dark walnut, was a treasured possession initially purchased by her father specifically for her grandmother's letter-writing.

With a steaming cup of tea, she leaned back and took a deep breath, feeling contentment and comfort for this moment of calm to escape from the demands of her usual scholarly schedule. Within the confines of this quiet and endearing room, it was as though her grandmother, who had always been an essential guide in biblical historical matters, was right there with her. She and her grandmother found solace and inspiration in their passion, connecting deeply with this remarkable woman's story. Seraphina suspected that her grandmother knew that one day, she would want to use her unique talents to uncover as many details about Mary Magdalene as possible. They had both marveled at her ability to endure countless trials and tribulations while still emerging as a prominent figure in the annals of Christian history. Sitting in her grandmother's chair, surrounded by the memories they shared, she felt a sense of deep gratitude as she closed her eyes to whisper a quiet and endearing thank you, believing her grandmother was smiling down on her with pride.

Immersed in this long-awaited moment, she placed her box of collected material nearby to begin. As she started going through the relevant material collected, she delicately embraced the pages of her meticulous Biblical notes on Mary Magdalene. Nestled in the chair's soft cushions, she sought with her trained eye precious fragments of information like hidden treasures awaiting to be discovered. Completely engrossed in the pages, she was oblivious to the gentle, rhythmic ticking of an antique clock on the wall. The world around her seemed to blur as if fading into the distance, while the passing of time became insignificant. Her eyes meticulously scanned her neatly arranged notes, tracing the inked words with unwavering focus. At the same time, the golden hue of the rising morning sun painted delicate shadows across the room, illuminating the aftermath of the rain's gentle departure.

As Seraphina immersed herself in her notes, she felt a sudden shiver coursing down her spine, sending an unfamiliar feeling through her body. Simultaneously, the air seemed charged while a peculiar aroma of fragrant oils gently teased her nostrils. The alluring scents of spikenard, sandalwood, and myrrh gracefully wafted through the air, their delicate aromas intertwining. As she sat there, a wave of confusion washed over her, for the room and all its contents began to dissolve like wisps of smoke. The room's familiar walls and furniture began to fade away, replaced by an ethereal landscape, causing Seraphina to exclaim, "Oh my goodness!" Enchanting lights materialized around her, flickering and dancing in a mesmerizing display. They illuminated the room with a vibrant glow, casting playful shadows that seemed to come alive. She felt herself drawn deeper into this enchanting realm, where the air shimmered with magic, and the possibilities of fantasy unfolded around her. A captivating sight was slowly beginning to emerge, gradually revealing a stunning horizon that seemed to defy reality. Colors exploded, dancing in a dazzling array of hues, leaving her breathless. At that exact moment, another breathtaking sight began to unfold as Seraphina witnessed countless rows of olive trees appear, their emerald leaves catching the sunlight and shimmering like rare and precious gems. She was where the ordinary ceased to exist, blurring reality's boundaries. A feminine figure slowly materialized from this otherworldly realm when things seemed beyond comprehension. The figure became more apparent with each graceful step toward Seraphina, leaving her gasping as she struggled to comprehend the extraordinary sight before her. The woman's hair floated elegantly around her head while her face seemed to emerge from behind, floating papyrus pages and ancient books she held tightly. Seraphina found herself most inexplicably spellbound by the woman's entrancing eyes. They seemed to embody the vastness of the cosmos, reflecting the world within small celestial orbs as if the universe itself were captured within them. Through the swirling ancient pages, Seraphina could see that her face was soft and gentle, with lines around her eyes that revealed the wisdom gained from life's trials.

The air in the room felt heavy with the faint scent of long-ago knowledge, mingling with the quiet whispers of long-held secrets. Seraphina leaned closer, trying to discern the messages hidden within the faint echoes of the books she carried. Wholly absorbed in the image before her, she felt a warmth and reassurance that drew her closer. A faint sense of familiarity lingered in the air, accompanied by a scent that nudged at her memory. The atmosphere crackled with an indescribable vitality, as if tiny sparks of electricity playfully danced around the room. Amidst Seraphina's swirling emotions, a vivid memory resurfaced, transporting her back to an excavation site. She wondered if this was the same woman who had held ancient parchments and books she encountered years ago. The eyes that stared back at her from the shadows of her room today seemed hauntingly familiar. Completely mystified, she sank deeper into her grandmother's chair. The pages of her notes seemed to vibrate with unexplainable energy, coming to life in a way that was impossible to articulate—time appeared to dissipate into nothingness as she looked up to gaze into her visitor's soulful eyes. Then, taking a deep breath before speaking softly, barely above a whisper, she mustered the courage to say, "Mary, I believe it is you, the woman I have cherished from afar; your life and words have bloomed within my soul, becoming a cherished gift. I have longed to understand you and your journey, and I am here, ready to listen to anything you wish to share." Looking deeply into one another's eyes, they shared a moment where no words could capture the intimacy.

Locked in a profound gaze, their eyes spoke volumes, transcending words. As moments slipped away, the figure's once sharp features began to blur, like a delicate watercolor fading under the gentle touch of raindrops. There was a silence in her presence, no words escaping her lips, while the air around her was filled with electrified energy.

 In this ethereal scene, the clock's ticking went unnoticed, drowned with time, as the room slowly returned, leaving only the sweet scent of fragrances lingering in the air.

Seraphina felt her senses overwhelmed as the entire experience penetrated her very being, evoking a cascade of newfound emotions that she had yet to comprehend. Mary Magdalene was precisely as vibrant and beautiful as Seraphina had always imagined. As she gazed into Mary Magdalene's eyes, they appeared almost ethereal, pulling her in like a magnet. Staring into them made her feel as if time stood still, transporting her to a place where all the answers to life's mysteries were within reach.

The trials that Mary had faced, etched in the subtle lines of her face, spoke volumes. They revealed a past marked by adversity yet illuminated by the triumph of healing and extraordinary strength. Seraphina could sense the richness of her journey—a narrative woven with threads of struggle and resilience that had shaped her into the remarkable woman before her.

Seraphina's fingers tingled with anticipation as she yearned to uncover everything she could about Mary's life. A flurry of questions raced through her mind, swirling like leaves caught in a storm. She pondered the significance of the scroll pages and the books Mary held closely.

Mary Magdalene's story was like a tightly sealed book, its intricate contents shrouded in mystery. During her extensive scholarly research and journeys, she meticulously gathered a variety of fragments, notes, and copies of ancient scrolls, a testament to her dedication and curiosity. Every discovery felt like collecting scattered pieces of a complex puzzle. Yet, despite the excitement of these revelations, the larger narrative remained shrouded in uncertainty, elusive, and just out of reach.

Seraphina reminded herself that men were the dominant force during Mary Magdalene's era, and women had little opportunity to shine. However, one quality seems to have set this woman apart—something extraordinary that made her stand out despite being a woman. A sophophile at heart, her profound love for knowledge, truth, and wisdom was remarkable. It was coupled with her unwavering spirit, adding a sense of resilience to her pursuits. Combined with his masculinity, the presence of feminine divinity would create a powerful force, ultimately resulting in the birth of the Christian faith through Jesus Christ.

In the biblical narrative, Luke 7:36-50, their journey begins when Jesus receives an invitation to share a meal at the house of Simon, a Pharisee. As the evening unfolded, an uninvited woman called Mary the Magdalene from the city of Magdala made her way into the gathering. She tenderly carried an alabaster jar filled with fragrant myrrh in her hands. The serenity in Mary Magdalene's eyes must have contrasted sharply with the judgmental glances of the Pharisees.

With tears streaming down her face, Mary positioned herself behind Jesus as she poured the contents of her jar onto him. Her fingers delicately intertwined with her flowing hair. She used her tresses to dry his feet as her soft weeping filled the room. In a gesture of utmost reverence, Mary anointed him with the precious ointment that must have filled the room with a rich aroma, adding an ethereal touch to the sacred moment. The Pharisees criticized Jesus for allowing this woman to touch him and waste expensive oils used that achieved money to help the poor. They believed that if Jesus were indeed a prophet, he would have known what kind of woman she was - a sinner. Despite their objections, Jesus welcomed Mary Magdalene's gesture and proclaimed to the others, "Leave her alone. Why are you bothering her? She has done a lovely thing to me. You will always have the poor around, and you can help them whenever you want, but you will not always have me around. She did what she could; she anointed my body for burial ahead of time. I tell you the truth: wherever the good news is preached throughout the world, what she has done will also be said in her memory." Seraphina felt that this particular event beautifully depicted the qualities of Mary Magdalene, such as her humble nature, pure love for Jesus, and her initial devotion to him. It also emphasizes Jesus's teachings of forgiveness and compassion for all, which are remarkable and inspire the values she felt we all wish to live by. She was also reminded that Mary's story is known worldwide, just as Jesus proclaimed.

Their first encounter is a remarkable tale that captures Seraphina's imagination and transports her to a distant time long ago. As she read the biblical account, she could almost feel the weight of history and the air thick with the scent of antiquity. It's as if she was there hearing the sounds of Mary's determined footsteps as she walked into the Pharisee's home to seek knowledge and wisdom from the revered teacher. It's a story that also reminded her of the opulent legend of the Queen of Sheba, who traveled from afar to witness the renowned sagacity of King Solomon. She believed that these women's unwavering strength and determination to seek enlightenment demonstrated the extraordinary power of feminine resolve, serving as an inspiration to everyone.

Suddenly, Seraphina was surprised by her grandmother's words that came to mind. Playfully, her grandmother had condensed the unforgettable first encounter between Mary and Jesus, relishing the vivid imagery. She wondered how many women would enter a home gathering uninvited—especially those who likely wouldn't have received an invitation in the first place—only to pour expensive oils on one of the guests and then dry them off with her hair. With a twinkle in her eye and a playful smile dancing on her lips, her grandmother leaned in and said,

"Now, that lady. Had some serious chutzpah!"

Seraphina's smile widened as she listened to her grandmother's words. Chutzpah indeed! And then there was Jesus, who seemed to have foreseen her intrusion with his profound wisdom and spoke tenderly; his words carried the weight of reverence, praising her for the beautiful act she had committed and remarking that what she did would be recorded in memory as indeed it has been written in our bible for generations beyond. Overcome with emotions, Mary wept softly, each tear a testament to her longing to connect with this great teacher. Everything happening was being expressed from the depths of her soul. Seraphna's notes indicated that the pages in Luke were believed to be meticulously penned by Luke, a devoted companion of Paul. They gracefully unfold this story, and one cannot help but be engulfed by the mesmerizing aura of love and unfiltered emotion that saturates every word. She could feel her feelings rising like a tide ready to burst, struggling to be contained. She thought that perhaps this initial encounter between Mary and Jesus had already been ordained as if the celestial bodies had woven their cosmic tale long before.

In Luke 10:38-42, Seraphina noted that Mary Magdalene's focus was from the beginning wholly absorbed in listening to the Master and his teachings. When her sister Martha appealed to Jesus, saying," Master, do you not care that my sister has left me to do all the serving by myself? Tell her that she should help me." The Master answered, " Martha, Martha, you are worried and upset by many things, but only one thing is necessary. Mary has made the better choice, and it will not be taken away from her." From the beginning, it was clear that Mary had a notable quest for knowledge and wisdom. She found in Jesus a teacher who possessed all the wisdom and knowledge she sought, perhaps making her his greatest admirer.

Among the accounts featuring Mary in the Bible, Seraphina identified the narrative of Lazarus as the most widely recognized and significant one. Seraphina's biblical notes indicate that Lazarus is recorded as the brother of Mary and her sister Martha. Jesus appeared to have a strong bond with their family, and they deeply loved one another. When Lazarus fell ill, his sisters sent for Jesus. According to the Bible, Jesus arrived four days after Lazarus had been laid to rest in a tomb. As Martha hurried to meet Jesus, she expressed her belief that if he had been there, her brother would not have died. Jesus reassured her that Lazarus would rise again, but Martha thought he was referring to the future resurrection. However, Jesus proclaimed himself as the resurrection and the ultimate source of life. He declared that all those who believe in him will endure eternal life, even beyond death. When Mary came and prostrated herself at Jesus' feet, sobbing, Jesus calmly inquired, "Where have you laid him?"

The account of Lazarus's miraculous resurrection was one of those events that left Seraphina in awe; she struggled to grasp its magnitude fully. She couldn't help but ponder whether Lazarus had died and, if so, how anyone could assimilate such an extraordinary occurrence into one's consciousness. As she tried to re-imagine the scene, she could barely envision the gripping sight of Lazarus emerging from the tomb, accompanied by gasps and whispers of others in attendance. The overwhelming sense of shock and wonder that would have enveloped all those present was sure to have left an indelible mark, making it inconceivable for anyone to emerge from such an experience unchanged. It was an astonishing event that defied description.

Seraphina noted that Mary, in an act of great humility, had knelt before the man called Jesus Christ not once but twice in an awe-inspiring display of deep love and devotion. The magnitude of her reverence towards Jesus must have left a lasting impression on those who were fortunate enough to bear witness to these sacred moments. Her unwavering devotion to Jesus is a powerful example of what Seraphina felt it meant to live a life of true faith and unconditional love. The emotions are so profound that words would not suffice in capturing the depth of feelings that those present must have experienced.

This story's setting was a small town called Bethany, enveloped in adoration and serenity. Here, Jesus would later transform and rise to the heavens, making Bethany a cherished place between the Calvary's crucifixion site and the town where Lazarus rose from the dead.

Seraphina's notes provide a wealth of information about Mary's role in Jesus' ministry. According to her notes, Mary was not only one of the financial supporters of Jesus' ministry but also a prominent figure among the group of women followers. In the Synoptic gospels, Mary is indicated as the most important woman in the group, just as Simon Peter was among the male apostles. This highlights the importance of women in Jesus' teachings and ministry, as mentioned in Luke 8:1. According to revealing biblical notes, Mary Magdalene and other women like her played a crucial role in Jesus' ministry by providing the necessary financial support. These women were affluent, and their contributions were instrumental in ensuring the success of Jesus' teachings and spreading his message.

She could easily imagine the women as undoubtedly instrumental in providing the necessary financial support for the ministry and bustling about meticulously planning and organizing meetings and meals. Their unwavering dedication to ensuring every detail was taken care of, from the smallest logistical detail to the spiritual well-being of the apostles, was essential to the success of Jesus' ministry. Despite being largely unrecognized and often relegated to the background, these women were the silent but powerful force behind the scenes, without whom the ministry may not have flourished as it did. Jesus himself admiringly acknowledged them and treated them with equality.

As Seraphina sat enveloped by the calm stillness of the room, she couldn't resist being consumed by her reflection of the ethereal aura of Mary Magdalene that appeared to persist within the room. She felt astonished that Mary's name appeared not once, not twice, but an incredible thirteen times in the Gospels, a true testament to her significance. Mary's name was mentioned three times in Matthew and three more in Mark's account, each recording her like a hidden whisper, while Luke contributed two more instances in the Gospel of John, as the weight of Mary's name was echoed five times. Seraphina learned that Mark 16:9 is like another hidden treasure that later added a 14th mention of the extraordinary Mary Magdalene.

Chapter Two

The Gospel of Mary

The hushed whispers of history permeated the room, and Seraphina felt that each account accurately documented the unwavering devotion of Jesus and Mary, their spirits fortified by an unbreakable thread. The biblical text painted a picture of the power of love that was not a mere fleeting emotion but a force capable of transforming lives. It possessed the power to heal the deepest wounds, like a balm for the soul, that flowed endlessly as a wellspring of inspiration that would continue to touch the hearts of countless generations.

As she shifted from her composed and reflective mind, her attention continued to be drawn toward various documents and pages before her. Among these papers were the ancient Gnostic Gospels, specifically copied for her on old parchment to provide a faint, musty scent reminiscent of the originals. With great care and attention, she ran her fingertips over the pages, ready to unveil any secrets they might hold from the past era.

The original pages were unearthed in 1896. The remarkable text, "The Gospel of Mary Magdalene," was written in Coptic and has since remained a subject of great curiosity and intrigue. Although its author remains unknown, it is widely believed to be the work of Mary Magdalene herself. Seraphina hoped that by studying this text, she could better understand this mysterious and intriguing figure and perhaps even uncover some previously unknown facts about her life and legacy.

It was in 1896 that this remarkable discovery unfolded amidst the ancient landscapes of Alhmin in Upper Egypt. Mary's gospel, written in the intricate script of Sahidic Coptic, emerged from the depths of sands, casting a mesmerizing sight upon the world. The bustling streets of Cairo witnessed its sale to a German scholar, Carl Reinhardt, as the vibrant sounds of a bustling market filled the air. The delicate pages whispered secrets of the past, carrying the faint scent of antiquity. Finally, the precious relic embarked on a journey to Berlin, its final destination, where it would continue to captivate the hearts and minds of scholars for generations to come.

Mary's gospel is a mesmerizing tapestry of history, immersing readers in a world of ancient wisdom. As the sole known female gospel, it shines as a precious gem in religious literature. Its pages carry the weight of curiosity, captivating scholars and enthusiasts eagerly exploring its words. There are hushed whispers of reverence surrounding its presence. Interestingly, Seraphina notes show that two additional fragments of the Gospel of Mary were discovered in separate Greek editions during archaeological excavations in Oxyrhynchus, Egypt, adding to its mystique. Despite the palpable excitement surrounding the remarkable discovery, the most complete copy of the Gospel of Mary, procured by the esteemed scholar Carl Reinhardt, but bears the blemish of torn pages. Regrettably, the absence of the initial six pages and four from the center renders it arduous to fully fathom this extraordinary artifact's profound depth and significance.

She wonders about the mysterious allure of the missing pages and the forbidden secrets they held. Yet, with its missing pages, Seraphina felt that Mary's Gospel remains a precious gem, invaluable to the world. Its worth transcends time, as its timeless words echo through the centuries, spoken by a voice long silenced nearly 2000 years ago. She firmly believed that within the cherished pages of our beloved bible, Mary's voice echoes with such gentleness that it seems to magnify the grandeur of the sky, amplify the splendor of the earth, and fill the air with a more delightful fragrance, ensuring her testament endures as an everlasting legacy.

In the dimly lit room, what remains of the gospel lay before Seraphina like scattered puzzle pieces, mere fragments of a forgotten whole. Scholars' brows furrowed in concentration have most widely accepted the date of these ancient texts to the 2nd century A.D. The Greek and Coptic translations, painstakingly completed, held the weight of centuries in their delicate pages.

As she settled into her grandmother's cozy, worn chair, the cushions enveloped her in a soft embrace. The faint scent of time hung in the air, mingling with the faint fragrance of faded ink. Eager anticipation coursed through her veins as if the room held its breath, anticipating the revelations soon to be unveiled.

With trembling hands, Seraphina gently held her cherished copies of "The Gospel of Mary" while envisioning the pages, the faint aroma of aged parchment filling the air. With eagerness, she began her voyage from page seven of Chapter Four, driven by the tragic absence of the preceding chapters and their enigmatic contents forever consigned to the depths of history.

Chapter Four of The Gospel

 Dialogue with the Savior.

. . . Will matter be destroyed or not?

22) The savior said, "All nature, all formations, all creatures exist in and with one another, and they will be resolved again into their own roots.

23) For the nature of matter is resolved into the roots of its own nature alone.

24) He who has ears to hear, let him hear."

25) Peter asks the Savior, "Since you have explained everything to us, tell us this also. What is the sin of the world?"

26) The savior replied, "There is no sin, but it is you who make sin when you do the things that are like the nature of adultery, which is called sin.

27) That is why the Good came into your midst, to the essence of every nature, in order to restore it to its root.

28) That's why you become sick and die, for you are deprived of the one who can heal you.

29) He who has a mind to understand, let him understand.

30) Matter gave birth to a passion that has no equal, which proceeded from something contrary to nature. Then, there arises a disturbance in its whole body.

31) "That is why I said to you. Be of good courage, and if you are discouraged, be encouraged in the presence of the different forms of nature.

32) He who has ears to hear, let him hear.

33) When the Blessed One had said this, He greeted them all, saying. Peace be with you. Receive my peace unto yourselves.

34) Beware that no one leads you astray, saying Lo here or lo there! For the Son of Man is within you.

35) Follow after Him.

36.) Those who seek Him will find Him.

37.) Go then and preach the gospel of the Kingdom.

38.) Do not lay down any rules beyond what I appointed you, and do not give a law like the lawgiver lest you be constrained by it."

39.) When He said this He departed.

Chapter Five of the Gospel.

1.) But they were grieved. Their tears flowed freely as they question, "How can we go to the Gentiles and proclaim the gospel of the Kingdom of the Son of

Man? If they did not spare Him, how will they spare us?"

2.) Then, Mary stood up from her seat, greeted them all, and addressed her brethren, saying, "Do not weep, and do not grieve, nor be irresolute, for His grace will be entirely you and will protect you.

3.) But rather, let us praise His greatness, she continues, for He is readied and shaped us into beings of purpose."

4.) As Mary spoke these words, she redirected their emotions towards the good, and they began to discuss the words of the Savior.

5.) Peter then turned to Mary and spoke, "Sister, we acknowledge that the Savior loved you more than the rest of us.

6.) Share with us the teachings of the Savior, "Peter implored, "the words that you remember, and we do not, that have eluded our hearing."

7.) And she began to speak to them in these words, "I will reveal to you that which has been hidden from you."

8.) With resolve, she commenced her account, "Listen closely. In a vision, I beheld the Lord and said to Him, "Lord, today I gazed upon You in a vision. He responded to me, saying.

9.) Blessed are you, for you did not waver at the sight Me. For where the mind is, there is the treasure.

10.) "I said to him, "Lord, how does he who sees the vision see it, through the soul or through the spirit?

11.) The Savior answered and said, "The
beholder does not see through the soul
nor the spirit. Instead, but the mind that
is between the two that sees the vision,
and it is..."

Pages 11-14 are absent from the
manuscript.

Chapter Eight of The Gospel

 Mary recounts her vision.

10.) "Desire said, `I did not see you
descending, but now I perceive you
ascending. Why do you speak falsely since
you belong to me."

 11.) "The soul answered and said, `I saw
you. You, however, did not see me, nor did
you recognize me. I served you as a
garment, and you did not know me.`

12.) "After the soul said this, the soul went away, rejoicing greatly.

13.) Again, it confronted the third power, which is called ignorance.

14.) "The soul approached the third power, called ignorance. The power questioned the soul, saying, "Where are you going? In wickedness are you bound, so do not pass judgment."

15.) The soul retorts, "Why do you judge me when I have not judged? I was confined, though I have not been the one binding."

16.) I was bound, though I have not bound.

17.) "I was not recognized," the soul continues, "yet I've recognized that the entirety is dissolving-both the terrestrial and the celestial."

18.) When the soul had overcome the third power, it went upwards and saw the fourth power, which took seven forms.

There are seven powers of wrath.

The first form is darkness

the second is desire.

the third is ignorance.

the fourth is the death wish.

the fifth is the fleshly kingdom,

the sixth, is foolish, fleshly wisdom.

the seventh is the angry person's wisdom.

19.) These are the seven powers of wrath.

20.) They asked the soul, "Whence do you come, slayer of men? Or where are you going, conqueror of space?"

21.) The soul answered and said, "What binds me has been slain, and what turns me about has been overcome.

22.) And my desire has ended, and ignorance has died.

23.) In an eon, I was released from a world, in a type from a type, and from the transient fetter of oblivion.

24.) From this time onward, I shall attain to the rest of time, of the seasons, of the eon, in silence."

Chapter Nine of The Gospel

25.) When Mary said this, she fell silent, since the Savior had spoken this much to her.

26.) But Andrew answered, addressing the assembly of brethren, "Discuss what you feel about her words. As for me, I find it hard to believe that the Savior would have spoken such things. Certainly, these teachings are strange ideas."

27.) Peter, answered, and spoke concerning these same things.

28.) He questioned them about the Savior, "Did He really speak privately with a woman, and not openly to us? Are we to turn about and all listen to her? Did He prefer her over us?"

29.) Then Mary wept and said to Peter, "My brother Peter, what do you think? Do you think I have thought this up myself in my heart, or that I am lying about the Savior?"

30.) Levi intervened, rebuking Peter: "Peter, your temperament has always been hot-tempered. Now I see you contending against this woman much like adversaries do. But, if the Savior made her worthy, who are you indeed to reject her? Surely, the Savior knows her very well." That's why He loved her more than us. Rather than that. let's be ashamed and put on the perfect man, and separate as He commanded us and preach the gospel, not laying down any other rule or other law beyond what the Savior said."

And when they heard this, they began to leave and go forth to proclaim and preach.

Seraphina's heart swelled with awe and wonder as she reached the final words of the Gospel of Mary. The profound depth of the text, accompanied by its vibrant richness, had etched itself into her memory, leaving an indelible mark. As she sat in the tranquility of her room, the scent of aged parchment filled the air, heightening her senses. She pondered the possibility that these words were penned by Mary Magdalene herself centuries ago.

The atmosphere in the room was thick with the lingering presence of her visitor, as if their essence had woven itself into the very fabric of the space. The fragrance of the oils continued to drift through the air, rich and soothing, wrapping around Seraphina like a warm embrace. This experience had ignited a symphony of sensations within her, awakening feelings of enlightenment and a humbling awareness of her place in the world. It was a moment steeped in profound personal reflection, a poignant reminder of the extraordinary ability of Mary's teachings to ignite a spark of introspection and deep contemplation within the soul.

She could easily conjure up an image of a highly skilled and dedicated scribe, wholly absorbed in his task of recording Mary's

Gospel. At the same time, the origins of his authorship remain a mystery, adding an element of intrigue to the narrative. Seraphina imagined the room would be dimly lit by the soft glow of a flickering candle, the air filled with the smell of aged parchment and small jars containing the earthy scent of ink. She envisioned the scribe sitting hunched over a small table with his worn leather apron draped over his slender frame. The rhythmic scratching of the quill against the papyrus would fill the air, accompanied by the occasional gentle tap as he dipped it into the well of ink. His hand, steady and practiced, would glide across the page with such precision that each stroke would seem to dance upon the surface. The weight of history and the weight of the words he would carefully inscribe were palpable in the room, as if the essence of time had settled on his shoulders. Seraphina thought that this act of creation, this delicate dance between pen and paper, would not be merely a task but a masterpiece in progress, destined to endure the test of time. The creation of the Gospel of Mary Magdalene, a rare and precious treasure, was written as an authentic account of the teachings of Jesus witnessed by one of his closest followers. Weathered with age and imbued with the musty scent of ancient parchment, the gospel was as ancient as any of the Christian bible gospels. Yet, Seraphina was reminded that it was almost lost to history, making its rediscovery a significant event in the spiritual and historical narrative.

Seraphina's notes reveal that in the 4th century, an edict whispered in hushed tones was sent to destroy all copies of this gospel, fearing it would undermine the church's authority. The sound of crackling flames and the acrid smell of burning pages filled the air as the order was carried out. However, amidst the chaos, brave and rebellious monks, their hearts pounding with defiance, stood firm and refused to obey the order. In the dim light of their secluded chamber, their fingers caressed the delicate pages, filled with ink marks that whispered of divine wisdom. Seraphina could only acknowledge their disobedience and spiritual bravery, which prevailed. Thanks to their unwavering dedication, this remarkable gospel is now the only one written from a woman's perspective.

She felt that the four missing middle pages would have contained the answers to what could be the most significant questions we could ever know. Mary asks Christ, "So, now, Lord, does a person who sees a vision see it with the soul or with the spirit?" We only have the first part of his answer, which is this provocative yet cryptic start: "The Savior answered, 'A person does not see with the soul or with the spirit. Rather, the mind, which exists between the two, sees the vision, and that is what . . ."

Seraphina's inquisitive and capable mind immediately was directed to Mary's essential question, "How do we see the vision?" Mary's thought echoed softly in her mind as she pondered the significance of perception. The answer to this question seemed elusive, as if some unseen spiritual authority had veiled it. The scent of uncertainty hung in the air, making Mary's question all the more crucial to answer. Seraphine firmly believed the answer was concealed due to the significant risks of uncovering it. However, if we dare to open our eyes and truly see, we'll discover a breathtaking panorama of inner wisdom awaiting us, like a vivid and enchanting tapestry. She thought about the gentle whispers of truth surrounding us like a symphony of delicate melodies filling the air. The undeniable fragrance of possibility lingers, inviting us to breathe in the essence of divine presence.

As Seraphina embraces this idea, a sense of clarity washes over her, as if a warm sunbeam illuminates our path. With each step, she feels the ground beneath our feet, solid and reassuring, would guide us toward a life filled with purpose and authenticity.

Ultimately, she understands that the power to shape our reality resides within us, like a hidden gem waiting to be discovered. A symphony of possibilities dances in the air, filling her ears with sweet melodies of endless potential. The scent of opportunity lingers, intoxicating the senses as we reach out to grasp it. With each breath, she could feel the exhilarating rush of empowerment, knowing that we hold the key to creating the life we truly desire.

Looking through her research, Seraphina finds no words to describe when Mary entered the room, as the text only states that she "stood up." Since the early part of the text is missing, She assumes that she was likely there from the beginning of their meeting. Although still unfinished, the text is a remarkable treasure that captivates her senses. She is overwhelmed with pride as she witnesses Mary Magdalene's graceful presence in words, emanating authority amidst the disciples' palpable fear. The scene is vivid as Seraphina's heart swells with admiration for this firm and courageous woman, evoking a sense of respect for her strength and resilience. The disciples fear they will be compelled to suffer the same fate as the Risen Savior. It is their fear that shows they have misunderstood the teaching of the Savior, who taught that the deliverance from the body resulted in the removal of suffering and death.

Mary, however, intervenes, and it is compelling to see how she supports her companions, assuring them that the Savior will always be there to protect and guide them, leaving Seraphina with a greater sense of admiration and pride in Mary's leadership. Mary quickly assumes the dominant role of the disciples and reminds them that the Savior has prepared them. She could almost feel the weight of the room and sense the tense atmosphere as Mary spoke with such conviction and authority. Her act of speaking out during a time when women were often silenced and disregarded is genuinely remarkable. To take on the responsibility of pulling the disciples together required a great deal of courage and determination. Nonetheless, she accepted this role with dignity, humility, and grace—the Apostle among the Apostles. The role granted her as Jesus after the resurrection appointed her to go and tell the others that she had seen him and where they would meet. John 20: 11-18

Seraphina also found in the Nag Hammadi non-canonical Gospel of Philip that Mary Magdalene is portrayed as Jesus's favorite disciple and that he often kissed (the word "kiss" is incomplete and damaged) her on the mouth," which, of course, would immediately seem to imply lovers. However, in her notes the "kiss" could also be simply a greeting or speaking in Gnosticism that would suggest a kiss serves as a conduit for transmitting the essence of the spirit and knowledge. It is believed that the act of kissing symbolizes a profound spiritual connection rather than a physical desire. You forge a bond beyond mere physicality when you kiss someone with secret knowledge, leaving the term "kiss" as an open interpretation and its underlying intention. Still, in Seraphina's mind, the relationship between Jesus and Mary was profound and deep.

As Seraphina read through Mary's words, she felt an overwhelming admiration and reverence for this remarkable woman. When her fingers traced the words on the page, she could feel the presence of this extraordinary woman who defies the boundaries of time and space. A surge of inspiration filled her heart as she marveled at Mary's unwavering commitment and strength that continues to inspire generations. If the Bible is to be believed, then not only did she bear the burden of uniting the disciples, but she also had to stifle her own emotions, feeling the weight of her heartache and anguish after witnessing the merciless crucifixion of the man she cherished. Amidst her sorrow and agony, she persevered, determined to console others and restore their hope. The air must have been filled with the weighty aroma of sorrow, accompanied by the lingering traces of tears held back. Seraphina struggled to fully grasp the enormity of what Mary had experienced. Still, she couldn't help but deeply admire her unyielding strength to continue with grace and bravery that surpassed all human comprehension. She barely had time to take in her emotions, yet her courage was like the Phoenix rising from the ashes of her despair to ignite hope and courage in those who needed to hear the strengthening words to confirm Jesus's message.

Peter's disheartening words must have filled Mary's heart with sorrow, especially at such a difficult time. It was Peter, who had always been there for her like a brother. Her disappointment must have been profound with feelings of betrayal by his behavior towards her, for he had gone so far as to suggest that she had made up nonsensical words from the teachings of Jesus. He might have felt angry at her vision, interpreting it as a suggestion that Jesus favored her over the other women and male disciples. What must have saddened Mary the most was that Peter's actions seemed to imply that he viewed her as inferior and unworthy of the wisdom from Jesus that she had shared. As she wept, Seraphina couldn't help but feel gladdened by Levi, who came to her aid with great chivalry and grace while every tear she shed continued to water the seeds of resistance within her soul.

Through Jesus's teachings, Mary tells us that we are not sinful; we should not feel ashamed or unworthy of being human. She whispers to us the essence of our purpose. We are urged to turn inward, repeatedly finding solace in the whispers of our thoughts as we embrace our imperfections and boundless potential, embodying what it means to be a "true human being."

Seraphina can only be further astonished as Mary communicates and understands her revelatory vision of the soul and its demise when she shares this vision with the disciples. She never faltered, regardless of gender, to show leadership as a spiritual teacher with the wisdom of a woman who is said to understand everything of Jesus's teachings. Seraphina's heart ached as her eyes welled up with tears. The weight of sadness enveloped her like a heavy fog settled upon her soul. The air was heavy with the scent of injustice, a bitter reminder of the grave mistake that had been made. The haunting whispers of judgment and condemnation echoed in her ears, a sorrowful melody that lingered relentlessly. Seraphina could sense the weight of time bearing down on her as the historical stigmatization of

Mary as a repentant sinner and prostitute cast a somber shadow over her very existence, an enduring injustice that defied erasure. Scholars and artists alike would pen, paint, and sculpt through countless ages, creating vivid depictions of Mary steeped in sin.

Amid its concise nature, she cannot help but notice how Mary's gospel resounds with a powerful voice reverberating through the ages. It is a voice that exudes resilience and courage and refuses to be silenced or marginalized. As the words spill across the pages, they create a scene that tugs at the heartstrings, a poignant reminder that the fight for equality and justice is an ongoing struggle, echoing through the corridors of history and persisting to this very day.

Towering stacks of well-studied books surrounded Seraphina as she meticulously arranged notes in the serene stillness of the room, filled with scholarly intrigue. Her fingertips danced across each page of her notes as she embarked on her quest to retrace Mary Magdalene's ancient footsteps. She tried to imagine how the melodic cadence of Jesus' voice would have sounded; indeed, it was commanding yet filled with tenderness to speak words that could touch the core of a person's being. How fortunate it was for those who heard. She coveted the dream of a world where the possibility of love reigned supreme, where her heart could dance in a rhythm of pure love. She wondered if this was the world that Jesus and Mary envisioned.

She notes that in other uncanonized Gnostic texts, Mary is recorded as asking many more right questions. In Pistis Sophia, the master continually praises her, as her heart is said to be more attuned to heaven's kingdom than her brothers'. In the Dialogue of the Savior, she beautifully and accurately quotes the words of the Master. Still, throughout the translated scriptures in the Nag Hammadi Egyptian Library, she is continuously challenged as a woman.

As Seraphina sat there, lost in her thoughts, her mind was flooded with many questions that swirled around like a whirlwind. She could picture herself transported to a bygone era of Biblical civilizations where the air would be heavy with the enticing scent of exotic spices and fragrant oils, evoking a sense of nostalgia. She could imagine a bustling marketplace filled with a vibrant kaleidoscope of colors as her mind wandered into her imagined version of the past. Her surroundings grew hazy, like a distant memory, as if fading into the ethereal realm. The air seemed to shimmer with a delicate, soft, ethereal light that danced upon the wall. And still, there was that subtle fragrance reminiscent of spikenard, sandalwood, and myrrh.

The weight of her desire to unearth the truth behind Mary's story had become an unyielding force that pulled at the depths of her being. It had taken hold of her soul, refusing to let go and urging her to use her unique talents to unravel the mysteries hidden beneath the surface.

In a sudden rush of recollection, Seraphina's mind was filled with the vivid imagery of a scene captured by Father Henri Dominique Lacordaire around the mid-1840s. She could almost see the women, their faces etched with grief, as they gathered together after the crucifixion. The air was heavy with the scent of mourning as their delicate hair tresses cascaded down, gently caressing the cool floor. It was a solemn tribute, a poignant gesture of reverence towards the sacred altar of divinity. As she builds a larger picture of

Mary and her life, she can almost feel the weight of the countless pages of notes in her hands, each adding a new layer to her story.

Chapter Three

The Manichaean Psalms of Heracleids

In an earlier study, she vividly remembers The Manichaean Psalms of Heracleids. She can still visualize the ancient pages, their edges delicately worn with time, as she felt them with great anticipation. The words leaped off the page, filling the air with a melodious hum as if the very essence of the text had a voice of its own. The scent of aged parchment wafted through the room, mingling with the faint aroma of incense, creating an atmosphere of reverence. As Seraphina immersed herself in the verses, she found a remarkable passage that extolled Mary for her crucial role in gathering the last disciples. The poet described her as the "spirit of wisdom," or Sophia, and Seraphina couldn't help but feel a sense of awe at the profound significance attributed to Mary.

In the serene Fayyum oasis of Medinet Madi, these valuable relics were discovered in the 1920s. Seraphina could envision scholarly conversations unfolding while the air was filled with animated discussions woven with the whispers of voices and the delicate rustling of aged manuscripts. The melodic tones of Greek and the enigmatic whispers of Syriac were suggested as the possible initial tongues of Manichaeism. Once a prominent world religion founded by the revered prophet Mani in the third century, it resonated with a divine revelation he claimed to have received from an angel he called the twin. Bestowed with the title of the apostle of light, Mani's teachings spread across vast territories, stretching from the majestic landscapes of Europe and the aromatic scents of North Africa to the bustling markets of distant lands in Central Asia and China.

The room was suddenly filled with a powerful resonance as the memory of the sacred words from the Book of Psalms echoed through it. Seraphina couldn't help but recall their ethereal message, proclaiming that Mary, with her delicate net, was ceaselessly searching to capture the eleven who had gone astray.

Eager to refresh her memory, she flipped through the pages on her lap until she located the copies of the Psalm she wanted to reread. She could still vividly remember the weight of the original weathered parchment she had held delicately at her fingertips. Its fragile texture seemed to keep the secrets of the past, with fragments of a forgotten melody, incomplete words, and lines that created an air of mystery and fascination. The soft murmurs of whispered conversations must have blended with the gentle rustling of their robes swirling around the room.

A Song from the Manichaean

Psalms of Heracleides'

Mary, Mary, know me,

do not touch [me].

[Dry] the tears of thy eyes,

and know me that I am thy master.

Only do not touch me.

for I have not seen my fathers face.

Thy God was not taken away,

according to the thoughts of thy littleness:

thy God did not die,

rather, he mastered death.

I am not the gardener:

I have given, I have received the...,

I did [not] appear to you

until I saw thy tears and grief.... for me.

cast this sadness away

and perform this service.

be my messenger to those lost orphans.

Make haste rejoicing,

and go unto the Eleven.

Thou shalt find them gathered together

on the bank of the Jordan.

The traitor persuaded them to be fishermen

as they were at first and to lay down their
nets

which they caught men into life.

Say to them, "Arise, let us go,

it is your brother that calls you."

If they scorn my brotherhood, say to them

"It is your master."

If they disregard my mastership,

say to them, "It is your Lord."

Use all your skill and advice

until thou hast brought the sheep to the
shepherd.

If thou seest that their wits are gone,

draw Simon Peter....unto thee,

say to him," remember what I uttered

between thee and me."

"Remember what I said between thee and
me in the Mount of Olives;

I have something to say; I have none to
whom to say it."

Rabbi, my master, I will serve thy
commandment

in the joy of my whole heart.

I will not give rest to my heart,

I will not give sleep to my eyes. I will not
give rest to my feet until I have brought the
sheep to the fold.

Glory to Mariamme,

because she is harkened to her master.

she served his commandment

in the joy of her whole heart.

Glory and ...victory to the soul of the
blessed Mary.

This beautiful psalm is like a whispered treasure riding the winds of time, its ethereal melodies entwining Mary's soul, drifting like dandelion spurs, embraced by the salty breeze, journeying from sea to sea. Never to be lost, but to be carried like a celestial enchantment through the vast expanse of time. Serapfina felt that the Master's words must have radiated within Mary, illuminating her spirit with a brilliance that could rival the brightest stars in the night sky. They would ignite the flames of hope within even the most desolate hearts, forging a destiny that transcends the very fabric of time itself. Likewise, the Masters' unwavering faith in Mary urges her to journey to the eleven and alerts Serapfina's ear to question if she, Mary Magdalene, is meant as the twelfth.

Seraphina decided that this psalm gives a clue as to the reverence and passion with which Mary was thought of in the immediate centuries following the crucifixion. She was a mirror reflection of Jesus' teachings of Love, exemplifying the state of being that resonates deeply within our hearts to reveal the true essence of Love, our genuine authenticity. Throughout the available recordings of her life, she embodied the very meaning of love, the purest of all human emotions, revealing the true beauty and magnificence of the human spirit.

However, a noticeable change took place as the passing years and centuries continued. The narrative surrounding Mary Magdalene underwent a palpable shift in the fourth century. A solemn transformation occurred, significantly altering her importance within Jesus' ministry. Regrettably, her role in the ministry and Jesus' teachings diminished, and she was unjustly depicted as a prostitute. The air of injustice hung heavy as her significance faded into obscurity.

Seraphina records that there was never evidence of Mary Magdalene's life as a prostitute. However, it would take decades for this to be corrected. In 2016, Pope Francis finally elevated Mary Magdalene's status to "The Apostle of the Apostles," fitting in the Catholic, Eastern Orthodox, Anglican, and Lutheran denominations and would be celebrated on July 22 as a **feast day for Saint Mary Magdalene.**

It was announced as *the expressed wish of the Holy Father, Pope Francis, the Congregation for Divine Worship, and the Discipline of the Sacraments published a new Decree on the Solemnity of the Most Sacred Heart of Jesus, 3 June 2016, in which the celebration of Saint Mary Magdalene was elevated and inscribed in the General Roman Calendar with the rank of Feast. This decision, in the current ecclesial context, seeks to reflect more deeply upon the dignity*

Seraphina's research notes that religious teachings underwent significant transformations following Jesus's crucifixion. While sifting through piles of notes, conducting historical research, and examining scroll writings in Nag Hammadi, numerous changes in religious teachings that diverged from Jesus's original teachings were discovered. Over time, original teachings were gradually altered to accommodate the evolving beliefs of a newer generation and the influence of different individuals in positions of authority. One of the very notable changes was observed in the written records during the 4th century, specifically documented by the Roman Emperor Justinian.

In AD 53, Emperor Justinian, the then-ruler of the Roman Empire, stated, *"I blatantly and brutally removed the Teachings of reincarnation from the scriptures of Christian orthodox doctrines. For the first 500 years of Christianity, reincarnation was a vital component of Christian doctrines."*

Over the centuries, many religions have strayed from the original teachings of Jesus, and now she couldn't know the intent of the Roman Emperor Justinian or why he would change these teachings so drastically; however, that would have to be a matter for another occasion.

Serephina's notes indicate that there were over 400 books, of which 27 were selected by the Council of Nicaea in 325 AD to create the Bible we have today. This is when Constantine officially recognized Christianity as a lawful religion within the Roman Empire, endorsing the Roman Catholic Church and its scriptures to create our bible. More than 300 Bishops and

Deacons convened together. She couldn't help but smile, pondering the thought that they were naturally of male gender gathered to establish a creed that would serve as a guiding force in the development of the Bible. She could not find a record of the actual original creed. However, records show the short version as generally stated.

- Belief in one God, the Father, who created all things

- Belief in Jesus Christ, the Son of God, who was begotten by the Father before all ages

- Belief in the Holy Spirit, who proceeds from the Father and the Son

- Belief in the one, holy, catholic, and apostolic Church

During the meticulous process, over 27 books were eliminated, while the remaining books were edited to create a portrayal of Jesus that resonated with the deep convictions of the Catholic faith. Nevertheless, the written Bible endures as our paramount tome, emanating a radiant glow of faith, resonating with the persistent echoes of spiritual fortitude, and offering an unwavering compass to navigate the path toward a purposeful and devout life. The Bible is a timeless treasure, treasured by countless generations and families. Its rich history and profound teachings continue to inspire and resonate, making it a beloved companion through the ages.

Seraphina's research revealed that many gospels were overlooked and not included in the formation of the Christian Bible. This led her to realize that the gospels that were ultimately selected underwent alterations, edits, and embellishments to shape the Biblical narrative we know today. For example, could the story of Jesus walking on water be one of these embellished accounts? Nonetheless, she firmly believed that Jesus and Mary truly existed and that the extent of creative interpretation in narrating their stories was left for each believer to determine its significance, if any.

Seraphina theorized that embellishments may have been made over time to reinforce the beliefs and values held by early Christians. Despite these editorial changes, she firmly believed that Jesus and Mary existed as historical figures and created the story of Christianity that we cherish to this day.

Seraphina believed in the Bible's soothing effect, evidenced by the countless lives it touched as the Bible tells the remarkable story about a man with immense wisdom and knowledge dedicated to teaching all he knew to uplift humanity.

Seraphina refocused her thoughts on the room as she reflected on what she had learned about Mary Magdalene, her unwavering courage, and the women who followed Jesus. Joanna, Susanna, and Salome were just a few among the many women committed to his ministry. She could almost hear the rhythmic beat of their hearts resonating with his original teachings and feel the weight of their steadfast dedication, which continued to breathe life into the Christian narrative. To her, it was evident that Mary stood out among these women, as her story was the most detailed and deeply etched in our minds. These women were not just followers but support pillars, providing care and resources that helped sustain the movement.

Seraphina felt an insatiable yearning to delve deeper into the profound messages that Jesus had once shared with Mary, messages she believed held the key to understanding the very essence of love and compassion. She was captivated by the idea that Mary had cherished these teachings and longed for the world to embrace them. Each glimpse into Mary's life, from her humble beginnings in a small village to her pivotal role in the divine narrative, filled Seraphina with a mix of admiration and inspiration, adding layers of significance to the information she had recently uncovered.

As she sat in the dimly lit study, surrounded by towering piles of books and scattered notes, her fingers clumsily flipping through the myriad pages punctuated the room's silence. The meticulously organized notes served as a testament to her relentless pursuit of knowledge. With every page she turned,

Seraphina sought to refresh her memory, piecing together the intricate tapestry of insights and reflections illuminating Mary's journey and the profound legacy of Jesus's teachings. The echoes of her thoughts mingled with the soft rustling of paper, filling the air with an atmosphere thick with purpose and determination.

Chapter Four

Magdala

Seraphina found that history had recorded Mary Magdalene's birthplace as likely the village of Magdala—because several texts dating back to the 6th century A.D. mention this. She also noted that in the 4th century CE, Empress Helena, mother of "Emperor"

Constantine, arrived at the ruins of ancient Magdala and built a basilica over what she believed to have been Mary Magdalene's home, according to the stories of the local people. Later, in the 8th and 10th centuries A.D., the church, which was believed to be Mary Magdalene's home, was again recorded. Descriptions were written on ancient stone walls that could conceal whispered stories of centuries past. Later, in 1283, Burchard of Mount Sion stepped into the church where Mary Magdalene was believed to have lived. He spoke of the ethereal ambiance created by the dim light casting colorful shadows filtering through stained glass windows. The scent of aged wood and incense lingered, evoking a sense of sacredness. Burchard's heart swelled joyfully, his footsteps echoing softly on the ancient stone floor. Around ten years later, Ricoldus of Montecroce discovered the church and house still standing. Overwhelmed with happiness, he marveled at the resilience of these sacred grounds, feeling a deep connection to the past that transcended time. These were all recorded bits of history revealing the location of the home where Mary Magdalene once lived. So, to Seraphina, it seemed likely that Magdala was Mary Magdalene's birthplace and home.

Newly recorded in Seraphina's notes was that in 2009, deep in the heart of Galilee, a Spanish priest embarked on an extraordinary journey. He was busily working on constructing a religious retreat center and filled the air with the scent of anticipation. But then the sound of hammers hitting stone soon gave way to a surprising discovery. The workers, eyes wide with awe, stumbled upon ancient stone walls worn by time. As they explored further, their footsteps echoed through the passageways, revealing a hidden world. They had discovered the deeply buried remains of the ancient town of Magdala. Magdala was thick

with the weight of history, carrying the faint aroma of fish, remnants of a bustling fish market that once thrived there. This was no ordinary place; it was believed to be the sacred home of Mary Magdalene, the devoted follower of Jesus, and her family. In this hallowed location, the scent of the past mingled with the present, creating a unique atmosphere that evoked a sense of reverence and a profound connection to her ancient history.

During the excavations, a hidden gem was discovered - the remains of a synagogue from the first century. The site was found to be a treasure trove of knowledge and artifacts from the time when Jesus would have likely been teaching and preaching in the region. The site was filled with pottery, glass, and many bronze coins from the 1st and 2nd

centuries CE. One of the most intriguing discoveries of the excavation was the mosaics from the Herodian era. They also discovered a room that was used for storing Torah scrolls. In the center of the synagogue, a beautifully carved Magdala stone was uncovered. It is believed to have been used as a base for a reading table supporting the Torah scrolls. This odd stone depicted what experts believe to be the oldest representation of the Great Temple of Jerusalem. It also shows the oldest carved image of a seven-branch menorah. What a find and delight!

According to historical records, the Roman army was thought to have destroyed the town of Magdala in the year 70 A.D. while they were laying siege to the city. Based on these remarkable findings, it becomes evident that a portion of the town had miraculously endured. The sight of standing structures amidst the rubble ignited a glimmer of hope. Today, centuries later, as the excavation process continues, the remarkable remnants of the once beautiful and historically significant synagogue are gradually being unearthed. One of the most mesmerizing discoveries is the intricately crafted six-leaf rosette, its delicate design invoking the awe of the early synagogue. Moreover, as layers of dirt are peeled back, vibrant and partially preserved frescoes emerge, their vivid colors a feast for the eyes, revealing the captivating beauty of the once-beloved gathering place. Seraphina found it easy to imagine the exquisite, tiled floors, now unearthed, to have once felt the gentle touch of Jeshua and Mary's sandals, imbuing them with their sacred energy as they glided together gracefully across the tiles. As Seraphina stood amidst the ancient stones, a deep sense of awe washed over her as she contemplated the rich tapestry of stories and histories buried beneath that sacred ground. Each step she took felt imbued with the weight of the past as if the whispers of those who had walked here before were calling to her.

As her thoughts wandered, she dwelled on the enigmatic and revered presence that manifested in her room: a figure shrouded in mystery and intrigue, that of Mary Magdalene. She imagined that the delicate pages of forgotten manuscripts and the weighty tomes she carried held the secrets from her life and the life of Jesus long past—knowledge still waiting to be unearthed or revealed. The vivid imagery filled her with excitement and curiosity as she contemplated what truths might still be hidden. Could there be more to discover here, or might other findings await where history seems to whisper through the wind in places like Egypt? What secrets lay within the pages and books Mary clutched against her chest?

Could each page and book be a vessel of secrets longing to come to light?

Chapter Five

Echoes of Jesus and Mary Magdalene

Feeling the warmth and comfort of her room, Seraphina settled more deeply into her grandmother's cherished chair. The faded floral fabric, with its delicate patterns of pink and green, enveloped her as she sank into its well-worn embrace. The gentle creak of the wooden frame echoed in the room's quietness, adding a nostalgic charm and evoking memories of warmth and love.

Lost in thought, she gazed into the distance, the vibrant memories of the archaeological site flooding her mind, stirring a bittersweet wave of nostalgia from her trip to the dig site earlier.

 The grandeur of the scene was still etched firmly in her mind. The mosaic-tiled floors beneath her feet displayed a tapestry of soft gray tones. Intricate geometric patterns adorned the tiles, inviting her gaze to wander and explore.

Surrounding the synagogue space remain the sections of vibrant frescoes painted in red, yellow, and blue hues that once adorned the colorful walls. As she stood there, a hushed silence surrounded her, broken only by the distant echoes of her breath. With a heart filled with emotion, she offered a prayer, the words escaping her lips in a reverent whisper.

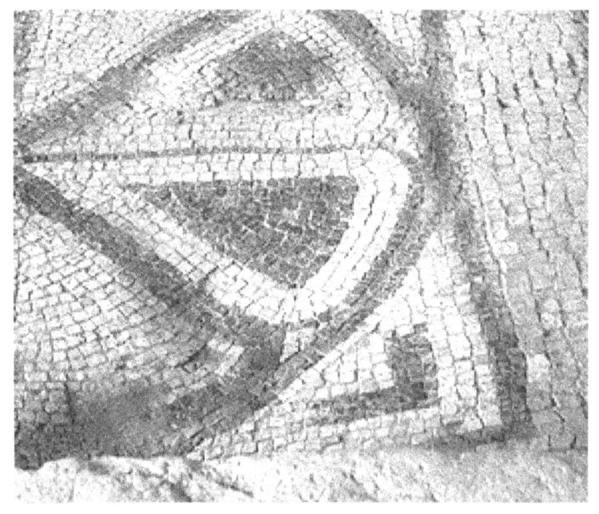

As Seraphina knelt, an irresistible urge washed over her, compelling her to touch the ancient stones before her. Her fingertips danced over the uneven surfaces of the unearthed mosaic tiles, revealing intricate patterns interwoven with history. With each gentle glide, a stunning assortment of vibrant colors came to life beneath her touch—rich blues, fiery reds, and golden yellows sparkled like jewels caught in the sunlight. The beauty of the mosaic sent electric shivers coursing through her body, awakening a deep sense of wonder and connection to the long-forgotten artisans who had crafted this stunning work of art. As her hand brushed against the surface, a swirling cloud of centuries-old dust was stirred up, sending dust particles floating through the air, catching the light and creating a mesmerizing display of shimmering sparks that seemed to come alive. The atmosphere felt charged with a delicate crackling, as if a supernatural force had been awakened from its slumber, awakening the latent energy lurking beneath the shadows. Layers of history seemed to hover just out of reach, begging to be uncovered and shared, as if the remnants of the past yearned for connection with the present. Within herself, she discovered a heightened awareness that allowed her to connect deeply with the ancient artifacts surrounding her. The air carried a subtle fragrance, gently reminding her of long-forgotten eras that embraced all her senses. In those captivating moments, as Seraphina crouched there, she could feel the dryness of the rough surface of finely cut stones from long ago beneath her hand. As she struggled to listen intently, Seraphina thought she could hear the ethereal whispers of the tiles, their delicate echoes wrapping around her in a symphony of forgotten past resonating in the air. These stories had traveled through time, carrying the presence of Jesus and Mary, their voices forming a gentle melody that stirred her soul. She was uncertain whether the mood and ambiance had conjured this imaginary tale for her, but at that moment, she only desired to embrace the richness of everything she felt in her heart.

With a deep breath, Seraphina slowly pushed herself upright from her cramped position, her heart pounding wildly in her chest as adrenaline surged through her veins. Her body swayed on the rough, uneven earth beneath her feet, making it more difficult to regain her balance and taking a moment to steady herself while carefully looking around. As she looked out across the exaction site, she observed crowds of people gathering, with their excited murmurs filling the air. Seraphina's eyes were immediately drawn to a woman centered in the crowd, who appeared to be cradling ancient books in her arms while also intently focusing on her. It felt like an unseen force drew their eyes together, creating an intimate connection between them and time that had somehow surrendered to allow this moment to exist. Seraphina, overcome by a flood of emotions, took a moment to collect herself and gently brushed away the tears that welled up in her eyes. Just as she believed she could begin to comprehend the situation, a gasp escaped her lips, her eyes widening in disbelief. The woman before her appeared to fade gradually, her figure becoming indistinct and shimmering until she finally dissolved into nothingness. Seraphina searched for any lingering trace of her but found none. The only remnant of the woman's presence was the lingering, hypnotic scent of spikenard, sandalwood, and myrrh that hung in the air. She stood in the dim light, confusion swirling within her as she grappled with the fleeting image of the woman. Was it real, or was it merely a figment conjured by her imagination, the warmth of the day and the thrill of the moment weaving a mirage in her mind?

Seraphina will never forget the day when all this happened, as it is deeply engraved in her memory. The next day became more challenging for Seraphina, as her heart felt heavy when she had to say goodbye to the peaceful "Sea of Galilee." The shimmering waves softly caressing the shore brought her a sense of calmness, almost as if she could hear the faint echoes of the fishermen's voices and laughter from long ago. She reached out to touch the cool water, feeling the gentle caress of the ripples against her fingertips, and a deep sense of connection resonated within her soul. The moments shared would remain etched in her heart forever and with a woman she knew she could never forget.

Later, she fondly admired the photographs at home, which captured the workers' diligent efforts. The sound of their excavating tools echoed in her mind as if she were still there. She could almost feel a sense of participation as each layer of soil was unraveled, always in hopes of revealing new relics of Mary's life as she journeyed alongside Jesus. Seraphina's relentless work schedule consumed most of her days, leaving little room for respite. Yet despite her packed calendar, she remained vigilantly attuned to the excavation team's progress, her anticipation mounting with each passing moment. The excitement of new relics surfacing filled her with thrill, yet her thoughts were consumed more by the enigmatic woman whose presence haunted her mind like a whisper in the breeze. The biblical account of Mary's life left her pondering the mysterious role of Mary Magdalene in Jesus' life and teachings. Questions lingered in the air as she continued to delve into the scriptures. Yet, amidst the uncertainty, she felt a profound sense of awe and reverence while contemplating the mysterious connection between Mary Magdalene and the teachings of Jesus. She ponders whether Jesus cast out or exercised seven demons or whether Mary Magdalene may have been able to understand Jesus' teachings better and overcome the seven demons of life through his teachings.

Seraphina could also easily understand that amidst the jealousies, hatred, and envy prevailing in the world, our day-to-day existence becomes a far more lucid journey when we free ourselves from these destructive emotions that obscure our path. In this tumultuous world, Seraphina understood that freeing oneself from destructive emotions was the key to a more lucid journey.

The missing pages of Mary's Gospel led Seraphina to believe that Mary's knowledge was far more advanced than recorded. Yet, there was a lingering sadness, a bittersweet reminder of why Mary's legacy was later diminished. Seraphina could almost feel the weight of history pressing upon her, the burden of a woman whose brilliance was overshadowed by the limitations of her time.

A touch of melancholy resonated deep within her, like a gentle ache in her heart.

She recognized that Mary Magdalene played a vital role in Jesus's ministry. In contrast, her role is downplayed in the Bible, leaving only glimpses of the authentic woman who would later inspire the most beautiful poems and psalms. Yet, Seraphina marveled at how Mary bravely accepted her role and worked within the boundaries set by society during her time in history. In her heart, she believed that Mary Magdalene was a woman who loved deeply, felt intensely, and grasped his teachings so effortlessly that she could envision a world filled with love while carrying on the vital work of the person she held most dear.

She thought about the other stories of a woman's love heard over and over throughout history. The story of Camelot came to mind as she remembered a widow's creation of a time called Camelot to keep the memory of a life that ended too soon. She knew that this was the astonishing power of a woman's love.

Then, the story of St. Joan of Arc came to mind, a story that can never be forgotten. Her extraordinary faith and unwavering courage shone brightly throughout her short life, culminating in a tragic yet powerful end. A young peasant girl Joan, felt called by divine guidance to lead her country during turmoil. Her remarkable conviction and determination inspired those around her, showcasing the incredible strength of feminine resolve. Despite insurmountable odds and eventual martyrdom, her spirit and beliefs remained unshakeable, leaving a lasting legacy that continues to resonate throughout history—the power of a woman and her faith.

Seraphina felt that Mary embodied that steadfast determination reminiscent of Joan of Arc, as she dedicated her life to spreading Jesus' message far and wide. Her unwavering commitment and faith inspired those around her and played a crucial role in ensuring that the Apostles' efforts would flourish. She passionately shared her faith with each encounter, fostering a sense of hope and purpose among the early followers. Her strength and faith served as a needed guiding light. Together, their committed dedication forged a sturdy bedrock, laying the groundwork for the nascent faith of Christianity.

At the same time, Mary had gracefully accepted that women were not recognized as societal leaders. Sadly, her own compelling words were ripped away from her gospel. Pages were torn away as if heresy and thought to be unfit for the eyes of those who held authority. While Jesus bestowed upon Mary a place of equality, at the same time, the world, steeped in patriarchal authority, refused to embrace that same delicate balance of trust and power. In contrast, Seraphina's heart swelled with admiration as she envisioned Mary Magdalene's unwavering presence at the crucifixion. In her heart, she could almost feel the agonizing sight of Mary surrounded by other women, their mournful cries filling the air. The smell of blood and sweat mingled with the suffocating scent of death. It must have been heart-wrenching for the women to witness such cruelty inflicted on someone they cherished so deeply. However, amid the overwhelming sorrow, she found solace in imagining the strength that resonated in Mary's voice. She could envision how Mary reassured the Apostles, urging them not to be afraid. She could even picture a gentle touch of Mary's hand as she spoke about the path the Lord had prepared for them all. It was a testament to the power and resilience of an extraordinary woman who comprehended life's enduring power and the soul's immortality.

Seraphina tried to imagine how Mary Magdalene's life could have been after the crucifixion. She believed that Mary was likely present at the Last Supper and continued to teach and heal after the crucifixion, as recounted in so many legends—legends that were a beautiful whisper of a long-forgotten truth echoing through time.

The medieval text known as the Golden Legends was a perfect example that speaks of Mary Magdalene's teaching and evangelizing in Provence, and later thought to have retired nearby to live in an Alpine Cave for 30 years. The cave remains available today as a tourist site and where the nearby small chapel of Sainte Pilon still sits, with an incredible view of the French Flora of the Sainte-Baume State Forest.

In that intimate chapel, Seraphina felt an overwhelming connection to Mary Magdalene. Her experience there was unlike anything she had ever experienced. As she stood quietly, looking out over the valley, the atmosphere seemed to have preserved and immortalized whispered prayers, suspended in time, reaching towards the heavens as if being forever engraved.

As she listened intently, the language of the prayers felt foreign, yet she marveled at how they flowed effortlessly with a blissful melodic lilt, transcending all understanding and inspiring a sense of wonder. The rhythm felt like a beautiful symphony, with each note striking a chord deep within her soul. It filled her with a profound sense of empowerment, peace, and awe that touched her heart to its very core. As Seraphina stood gazing out over the valley from the chapel, a profound sense of humility enveloped her like never before. She was uncertain if those around her shared her experience. For her, the vibrant world around her had just dimmed and dissolved, and had been replaced by an all-encompassing force of love. Love so strong it pulsed through her veins, leaving her dazed, with everything appearing as a shadowy blur.

She envisioned that this was the mystical place where Mary Magdalene had found solace among the angels. Seraphina knew this profound experience would stay with her forever, shaping her memories and emotions in ways she couldn't yet fully grasp.

Nearby in the town of Saint-Maximin-la-Sainte-Baume is a crypt in the Basilica of Mary Magdalene, claiming to house the skull and bones of Mary Magdalene. Seraphina's notes show that the relics believed to be that of Mary Magdalene were discovered in 1281. Charles II and Pope Boniface VIII agreed to build an impressive Basilica to house and honor the relics. The church, towering above the city, is visible from miles away. Seraphina had visited this area years ago as part of a research project. Back then, her main focus was to delve into the history of the Friars and their nearby hostelry, which the Dominican Friars managed. Interestingly, that was the place where she had stayed during her visit. Her stay there was very pleasant, with simple, basic rooms offering a fantastic calm and serenity. The food was delightful, and Seraphina discovered it one of her favorite places. Whenever she was in the area, she would often stay there as her work was easy to do in an environment that offered such a profound sense of peace, that it made her experience all the more nostalgic and productive.

The hike to the nearby Grotto of Sainte-Baume was a pleasant walk up a steep slope surrounded by incredible views. The cave was another hidden treasure that deepened Mary Magdalene's story.

As Seraphina strolled along, she quickly wiped away a tiny tear at the thought of this passionate and beautiful woman seeking solitude, prayer, and contemplation by living in a cave for many years. Could she have imagined Jesus returning to her, or were they never truly apart, united in spirit as they had been in the flesh? Seraphina couldn't be sure, but these thoughts touched her heart, evoking a mix of sadness and yet understanding that Mary had found a place of solace, connecting her with the heavens above.

With unwavering dedication, Seraphina had devoted her life to accumulating historical facts, meticulously piecing together the puzzles of the past, one fragment at a time.

She understood that genuine historical insight requires validation. While Mary Magdalene remains a fascinating and enigmatic figure in religious history, there remains very little detailed documentation of her life. While available scripture allows us to know her faith and passion, Seraphina felt that the most authentic portrayal of Mary Magdalene must be found within our hearts. Yes, she thought, we must seek her there. If we listen to our hearts, we will hear her continued voice.

As Seraphina walked along the wooded path, lost in her thoughts, memories of an afternoon at the Metropolitan Museum of Art in New York City flooded back to her. There, she came across a beautiful vial containing a tiny, delicate tooth believed to have belonged to Mary Magdalene. One of the many artifacts believed to be linked to Mary Magdalene scattered worldwide.

In a moment of whim, Seraphina pretended to envision ancient pages suddenly swirling around her, each revealing details of an afternoon tea where Mary's thoughts and words were shared and penned to be immortalized. Oh, how she longed for such a discovery, just like the many others who have written countless stories about Mary Magdalene, as our minds desperately yearn to know all the more about her.

She had found recorded legends rumored by Eastern traditions. In another recorded legend, Mary was thought to have been accompanied by St John to Ephesus, where she died and was buried. The town also has treasured bones believed to belong to Mary Magdalene. It was easy to believe that Mary had stayed and visited many places after the crucifixion.

Whatever happened would undoubtedly have been an arduous journey for any woman.

Seraphina noted that the pages of history vividly depict the male disciples meeting their tragic ends, like falling stars, until only John the Beloved remained, an exceptional survivor amidst the martyrdom and murders of the era.

Amidst the clamor and chatter, she focused her gaze on the ancient scriptures laid out before her as she traced her fingers delicately over the worn pages and held steadfast to her purpose – to reveal as much as she could support with documentation surrounding Mary Magdalene's life. She was devoted entirely to her purpose as a historical researcher - to seek out what she could through all the documentation she could find to create the picture of Mary Magdalene's life with Jesus.

However, what held significance for Seraphina was understanding the depths of Mary Magdalene's passion. She wanted to embrace   Mary's unwavering love and dedication to spreading *his* message. While the synoptic gospels show smatterings of her work after the crucifixion, her work in healing and teaching is incomplete and mostly lost. Still, with the continued devotion and work of the Apostles, we have the story of Christianity. Their sacrifices echo through the ages with Jesus's words of *His Father* etched into our souls. He gave everything, his very essence, his breath, his beating heart, to teach us that death is but an illusion. His crucifixion is his eternal message that there is no end: Jesus, who so loved, and his devoted companion, Mary Magdalene, who so believed.

Now sitting in her quiet room, Seraphina sat in silent reflection, basking in the gentle radiance of the sun as it bathed the room. The delicate aroma of spikenard, myrrh, and sandalwood still drifts through the air, intertwining with the melodic symphony of birdsong wafting from the trees outside. As she continued her thoughts, her fingers traced the delicate pages of an ancient Bible, searching for any tangible evidence of their marriage. She felt the marriage referred to in the bible likely could have been their marriage, but she could not find any direct scripture to substantiate this belief. So much was perhaps never written or was lost, changed, or even eliminated, including all the problems of various Aramaic, Greek, and Hebrew translations that created different versions of the same texts. Yet, deep within her, Seraphina knew that the love of Jesus and Mary stretched beyond the boundaries of this world, revealing the pure essence of Love. Within her heart, she could sense the sparkle in their eyes, hear the whispers of their shared secrets, smell the fragrance of their intertwined souls, and feel the warmth of their embrace.

Within the serene stillness of her room, Seraphina sensed she had discovered in Mary Magdalene as a sisterly soul. She felt a profound kinship in this profound connection, like a heartwarming embrace of sisterhood. She is a part of me, Seraphina thought, and I am a part of her, as we all are, sisters in soul and spirit: no womanly jealousies, but everything to embrace. Her spark glistens within each of our souls, yearning to be remembered. We cannot bear to let her go; our curiosity longs to uncover more and unravel her mystery.

Within that serene moment, a gentle breeze brushed against Seraphina's face as she closed her eyes; a faint scent of blooming flowers filled the air. The sound of distant birds chirping created a peaceful backdrop, enhancing her concentration. She recalled the subtle aroma of old parchment that seemed to emanate from the ancient manuscripts swirling around Mary's ghostly presence, almost as if revealing a treasure trove of undiscovered books that could hint at the literary wonders still awaiting exploration.

In Seraphina's room, it felt as if Mary were carefully guiding Seraphina's thoughts to unravel the profound understanding she longed for. To her, Mary Magdalene embodied a heart that glistened like the rarest gemstone, purified and untainted. A heart that exuded a sense of serenity, devoid of any trace of fear, jealousy, envy, or hatred, as if she was a mirror reflecting the divine teachings and heart of the Savior, she so unconditionally embraced. Seraphina believed that Mary's embodiment of pure love enabled her to fully understand and accept all of Jesus's teachings. She yearned for us to know the teachings and words of a man called Jesus, Roubonni, or Jeshua. She understood all the mysteries of the universe, we are still learning, and much more to be discovered through the scrolls, yet to be translated, and the work of all those so diligently translating and digging into the threshold of antiquity. The continued work of our era's dedicated minds piecing together the stories lost from our past. Seraphina felt a surge of emotion as she realized that Mary and the apostles were working to empower people to shape their destinies beyond death. As we strive to explore, grasp, and understand the mysteries of our world and life, we discover our purpose, and their work lives on through each of us.

Her voice quivered with raw emotion as tears welled in her eyes. Her hand, as delicate as a feather, tenderly rested on her chest, feeling the steady rhythm of her heart. She could feel a warm embrace enveloping her, like a comforting blanket in the cold. She whispered calmly, barely audibly, "Dearest Mary, I feel incredibly blessed to have found you. In the depths of my being, I have felt your unwavering presence as a constant companion in my heart. My heart tells me that when you departed from this mortal life, you transformed into a brilliant star seed, bursting forth in a cosmic explosion that painted the heavens with your radiance. Like a symphony of light, this celestial burst sparked the birth of countless extraordinary souls, their spirits aflame with the same passion you instilled to create a world crafted with boundless love, envisioned by your beloved Jesus and into every one of us. After two millennia, your story has remained a treasure, evoking a profound desire to explore the unwavering faith that led you to follow your beloved's message that would bring humanity salvation. Your message left no room for compromise, imploring us to forsake all else and embrace love as the core of our being, the purest essence of our souls. As our hearts are cleansed, we can truly embody the indescribable peace that surpasses all understanding. Beloved Mary, you were the embodiment of the feminine spirit of your time, shining a light on the path for generations to follow. We tread inspired by your luminous footsteps." Tears streamed down Seraphina's flushed cheeks, leaving glistening trails in their wake. She tenderly brushed them away with a delicate touch, her voice quivering and barely audible. Profound gratitude and humility lingered in the air as she softly uttered, "Thank you,"

The room was a sanctuary of tranquility, its stillness echoing softly. She sat in silence, basking in the reverence of the day. She was grateful for the shared moments, uncovering a life filled with humility, love, and wisdom and leaving a legacy for us to follow. The apostles told us the story of Jesus. The bible recorded their story and gave us the gift to enrich and guide our lives. As she reflected on her research, she came to the realization that she hadn't uncovered all the secrets of this remarkable woman; perhaps there were still more discoveries waiting to be made. Yet, deep down, she found herself questioning whether there was more to learn at this moment or if she had already grasped the most profound message: Love. Could Love truly be the timeless healer that offers redemption in every facet of life?

Seraphina could never forget the soft notes echoing prayers near the Chapel of Sainte Pilon. During these moments, she felt Mary's soul reaching out to bless the world. It was an experience she could never articulate as it was so deeply personal and intimate. In that sacred place, she heard the echoes of Mary among the celestial harmonies of the heavens, etching the valley in songs of peace and love for all who can hear throughout the ages.

She could not know what lay ahead. She believed the books held lovingly in Mary's arms symbolized the potential for discoveries, sparking a sense of intrigue and wonder in the sands of time.

She realized that while she was unaware of how Mary's journey ended, she was confident that Mary fulfilled her mission to spread the teachings of the man she loved and believed in. Regardless of what other documents might be discovered, she deeply understood that his teachings highlighted several profound principles. Foremost among these was the transformative power of love, which connected all beings. He spoke passionately about revering the earth and its natural beauty, urging respect and gratitude for the environment. This reverence extended to nature and the animals that share our world, emphasizing the interconnectedness of all living creatures. Furthermore, he taught the significance of treating each other with kindness and compassion, fostering community and mutual support. Above all, his lessons conveyed the promise of eternal life, instilling hope and a sense of purpose in those who followed his teachings.

As Seraphina settled into her softly illuminated room, the hours seemed to dissolve into a hazy blur. The warm glow of the amber-hued lamps cast delicate shadows on the walls, creating a cocoon of serenity that enveloped her like a cherished blanket. The fragrant scent of spinkard, myrrh, and sandalwood still lingered in the air, mingling with the soft rustle of pages lying in Seraphina's lap. She found herself lost in the tranquility, her mind swirling with profound thoughts about faith and purpose, each unfolding like a petal in the dawning light of understanding.

She felt strongly that the message conveyed when their eyes so profoundly met was to listen to our hearts where nothing is hidden. She marveled at the enticing promise of future translations of our lost past, books yet to be discovered, and the potential to translate damaged scrolls once thought to be unreadable. Advancements in new technology ignited a spark of anticipation for what lay ahead. With a sparkle in her eye, Seraphina felt a surge of excitement as she had been considering the possibility of a new research project. Recently, a library in Egypt approached her and expressed a keen interest in her insights and further research regarding the Cathars. This mystical group, known for its profound message of peace and spiritual freedom, is written within the works of Plato and follows the teachings of Jesus.

Seraphina couldn't help but feel that this project would explore another connecting pivotal moment in history, similar to Mary Magdalene's, as she contemplated the depth and complexity of this topic that lacked documentation.

Seraphina was uncertain if this would become her next project, as, at this moment, her heart was too consumed with love and admiration for Mary Magdalene's life and passion. Despite her uncertainty, she found joy in the idea of returning to France when suddenly she was jolted from her reverie by a deafening and piercing crash that echoed through the room, violently disrupting the serene atmosphere. It was as though the air around her had shattered, sending a surge of adrenaline racing through her veins. Her heart pounded in her chest, the sound a stark contrast to the tranquil moments she had been enjoying just moments before. The origin of the noise was unclear, as if it had materialized from thin air, and it shattered her sense of safety, leaving her eyes wide with alarm as she scanned her surroundings for the source of the chaos.

Startled and bewildered, her senses reeled as her wide eyes darted to the floor, where her beloved books—once neatly piled on her lapboard—had tumbled in a disarrayed heap. Their fall resonated like a thunderous cascade of thumps echoing against the wooden floor, each reverberation amplifying her bewilderment.

Annah's gentle voice could be heard echoing through the spacious house at nearly that exact moment, continuing to shatter the silence that had previously engulfed the room.

"Seraphina, darling, shall I start supper?" She called out while ascending the stairs.

The sound of her footsteps echoed throughout the house. Calling out again to her daughter, "Are you still up there reading?" Her worry grew as she neared her room and noticed a peculiar expression on her daughter's face. Concerned, she immediately inquired, "Seraphina, are you all right? What's the matter, my dear? You look as though you have seen a ghost." Her heart raced as she waited for a response.

Tinged with the nostalgia of the day, she could only speak gently to Annah. "It's not a ghost, Mother," she whispered, but a haunting melody reverberating through time—a melody that unveils the secrets of a woman we have all longed to know. The walls seemed to come alive in this room, pulsating with a quiet energy. I could almost see them expanding and contracting as if they were breathing. It was as if the room exhaled, whispering a long-ago tale I yearned to uncover.

Annah, sparkling with intrigue, leaned in closer, captivated by her daughter's words. "My goodness," she exclaimed, her voice brimming with curiosity. "You have had quite an extraordinary day. You must tell me every intricate detail."

"Mother, I can't wait to tell you about my extraordinary day," She exclaimed, her eyes sparkling with anticipation. "But my stomach is rumbling. I haven't eaten a thing all day." Their hushed footsteps floated in the air as they descended the stairs, each step filled with anticipation. The kitchen welcomed them with the tantalizing aromas of exotic spices, teasing their taste buds. Seraphina's senses came alive as she caught a whiff of spikenard, myrrh, and sandalwood lingering in the air. A smile played on her lips as she thought of the evening, no longer solitary but shared in the presence of an unexpected guest, creating a delightful tickle in her tummy.

Annah, filled with intrigue and wonder, could only reply, "All right, dear, shall we now warm up the Lasagna and add a crisp, fresh salad to go with it?"

"Yes, please, and I will slice the fresh strawberries Joseph picked for our dessert."

$\mathcal{A}$nd now,

As the sun dipped below the horizon, casting a warm golden glow over Seraphina's home, her story unfolded before us, stretching into the endless expanse of time. Her heart swelled with each step she took as if enveloping her in a timeless embrace. And so her story carries on, to be forever etched in our hearts.

Additional notes and pages in Seraphina's Journal.

The expanded version of the Creed of Nicene

O lord, thou hast searched me, and known me.

Thou knowest my downsitting and mine uprising, thou understandest my thought afar off.

Thou compassest my path and my lying down, and art acquainted with all my ways.

For there is not a word in my tongue, but, lo, O LORD, thou knowest it altogether.

Thou hast beset me behind and before, and laid thine hand upon me.

Such knowledge is too wonderful for me; it is high, I cannot attain unto it.

Whither shall I go from thy spirit? or whither shall I flee from thy presence?

If I ascend up into heaven, thou art there: if I make my bed in hell, behold, thou art there.

If I take the wings of the morning, and dwell in the uttermost parts of the sea;

Even there shall thy hand lead me, and thy right hand shall hold me.

If I say, Surely the darkness shall cover
me; even the night shall be light about me.

Yea, the darkness hideth not from thee; but
the night shineth as the day: the darkness
and the light are both alike to thee.

For thou hast possessed my reins: thou hast
covered me in my mother's womb.

I will praise thee; for I am fearfully and
wonderfully made: marvellous are thy
works; and that my soul knoweth right well.

My substance was not hid from thee, when
I was made in secret, and curiously wrought
in the lowest parts of the earth.

Thine eyes did see my substance, yet being
unperfect; and in thy book all my members
were written, which in continuance were
fashioned, when as yet there was none of
them.

How precious also are thy thoughts unto me, O God! how great is the sum of them!

If I should count them, they are more in number than the sand: when I awake, I am still with thee.

Surely thou wilt slay the wicked, O God: depart from me therefore, ye bloody men.

For they speak against thee wickedly, and thine enemies take thy name in vain.

Do not I hate them, O LORD, that hate thee? and am not I grieved with those that rise up against thee?

I hate them with perfect hatred: I count them mine enemies.

Search me, O God, and know my heart: try me, and know my thoughts:

And see if there be any wicked way in me, and lead me in the way everlasting.

1. Hannah noted in her paragraph that the word "Garment" in Mary's gospel refers to the garment that clothes us through life. The soul puts on the garment as it enters life and removes it when departing from the world.
2. Peter's hostility toward Mary Magdalene is also referenced in the Gospel of Thomas and the Pistis Sophia.

In Song of Songs 3:1-5, Hannah's eyes were captivated by the exquisite portrayal of a woman passionately seeking her lover. The words painted a vivid picture in her mind, as if she could see the gentle sway of the woman's dress and the softness of her heart. Hannah imagined the subtle scent of blooming flowers in the garden, mingling with tears from her heart. She imagined this enchanting description could be the reflection of the radiant Mary Magdalene, her heart still tender from the sorrow of the crucifixion.

Night after night on my bed

I dreamed of my lover.

I was looking for him

but could not find him

"So I shall rise and wander through the city, down the streets and through the markets.

I shall look for my lover."

I looked but could not find him.

The watchmen came upon me

as they patrolled the city.

I asked, Have you seen my lover?

No sooner had I left them

than I found my lover.

I held him, I would not let him go,

till I brought him to my mother's house,

to the chamber of her who conceived me.

Promise me, daughters of Jerusalem,

by the gazelles and swift deer of the field,

that you will not arouse me, will not
awaken my love,

until love is ready.

Johann A. Freylinghausen (1704) wrote 44

hymns and   published hymnals.   His *Geistreiches Gesangsbuch* (*Spiritual Songbook*), a hymnal with 1500 old and new songs known as "Freylinghausen's Songbook." One of his beautiful hymns was to Mary Magdalene.

Mary, to her Saviour's tomb,

swiftly at the early dawn;

spice she brought, and sweet perfume;

The Beloved One was gone.

The Magdalene weeping stood,

struck with sorrow and surprise;

shedding tears, a plenteous flood,

for the heart supplied her eyes.

Jesus, as if always near,

though too often unperceived,

came, a true leader to cheer,

asked to her soul, why she grieved?

What a change living words make,

turning our nights into day!

All who e'er weep for Life's sake

Additional references.

The Gospel of Thomas, usually dated to the late first or early second century, was among the ancient texts discovered in 1945. The Gospel of Thomas consists entirely of 114 sayings attributed to Jesus.[

Mary herself asks Jesus, "Whom are your disciples like?" Jesus responds, "They are like children who have settled in a field which is not theirs. When the owners of the field come, they will say, 'Let us have back our field.' They (will) undress in their presence in order to let them have back their field and to give it back to them". Following this, Jesus continues his explanation with a parable about the owner of a house and a thief, ending with, "Whoever has ears to hear let him hear."